A TRIO

SOMETHING THAT NEVER WORKS

ISHI AGGARWAL

Made with ♥ on the Notion Press Platform
www.notionpress.com

Mr. Ankit Gupta and Mrs. Heena Gupta

My parents have always been supporting me and have
motivated me every time I felt down.
Which was very helpful throughout my writing journey.
I would like to dedicate my work to both of them and
thank them with a lot of respect.

Contents

About The Author

Whenever I try to write a story, a short story; I end up crying and feel like I don't have any writing skills. I really want to write more books and go ahead in writing in the future. And then... while thinking the same, One day, a sudden thought hit my mind. It was not about anything else but... Stories and poems! As I have to write more books in the future too, for how long am I going to write poems? Poetry is ofcourse the most beautiful form of art. But for how it's going to be stretched? That was when I started writing this story. Just because I was bored, A thought came to my mind. It was to write a short story and enhance my writing skills. No one... Not even me, knew that this story will end up being in a book. With a lot of twists ofcourse!

For me, writing a story was a hard yet an enjoyable task. My favourite part was definitely writing 'About The Author' and sharing my 'experience' while writing my second book.

I'm 12 years old and I'm the youngest author of Shamli. I would like to suggest you all to read the book, understand the main message tried to convey through the book, try to understand the twists and suggest this book to others. So that they can get some motivation and feel good.

About The Book

I highly recommend you "A Trio: Something That Never Works". It is a fictional work by Ishi Aggarwal where she has beautifully used her passion of writing and has stated the friendship between three close friends who get apart from each other because of misunderstandings and highly because of the third one.

Three primary characters are present: one who is considerate of others, one who is conceited and melancholy; and one who is courageous enough to confront life's challenges.

Additionally, you will discover the history of the key characters, and eventually, you will discover what the future holds for them.

The third shade of the trio is compelled to learn and study. She wishes she could do something more creative, but is constrained by family rules. Despite being the only kid, she detested being treated like a princess but wishes to have everyone around her.

Later, one of the three becomes an expert in heart disease, another continues to work in the field of fashion design despite all the challenges, and the final member of the trio demonstrates the enchantment of colours through her artistic forms as she works to become an artist.

Also, this book isn't only a story based on friendship or something like that. It contains some life lessons to learn and even the key characters have a small motivational message to read. Do read it, enjoy it, learn from it, suggest it to others and feel good!

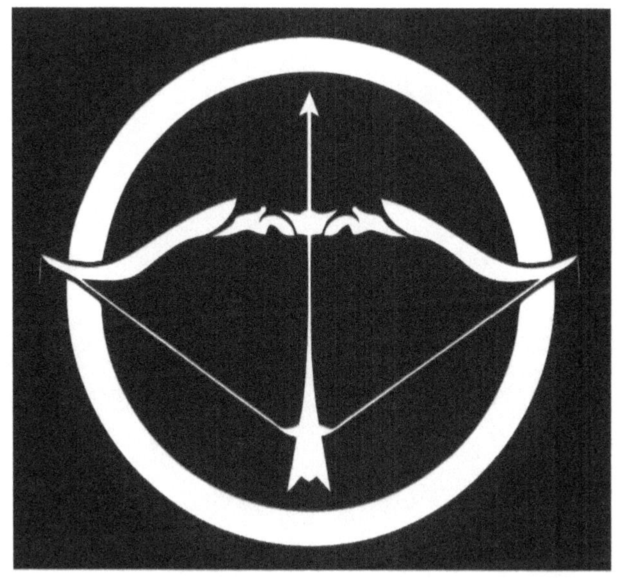

A book by
Penaaki

1
Introduction

Once upon a time, There were 2 girls, Shanaya and Ishanya. They both were 12 years old. They used to live in Jaipur (Rajasthan). They went to the same school. Both will be talked about below:-

"Shanaya"

She belonged to a middle class family. She had a dark complexion, short hair, a short height. Because of which, she was considered ugly. She used to be treated in a very ill manner just because of the financial conditions of her house. This was not enough. To Know her back story in detail, Turn to unit-2.

"Ishanya"

She belonged to a high class family. Being a rich; beautiful girl, She had a lot of arrogance and ofcourse a lot of fame. She was very beautiful but even very rude. Everybody wanted to be friends with her as she was beautiful and rich. But because of her arrogance, she used to say no to everyone and used to say, "I am alone, but happy." But no, even she had a back story. A sad one! Her back story will be talked about in unit-3.

"Let's talk about their friendship."

They both used to sit alone. As they both had no friends. They both didn't have friends for the different reasons and both used to sit alone and seperately. But one day what happened was, there was shortage of one bench as a new student took admission in the class. So, their class-teacher made both of them sit together. Because they were the only students who were sitting alone while others were sitting together with their friends. All the students used to laugh on Ishanya saying, "With whom are you even sitting?","You are sitting with such an idiot!","She will make you a stupid monkey."

These things hurt them both a lot. And specially Shanaya was badly hurt by these words. But then.. As she was very mature and emotionally strong, she didn't share her things with anyone. She thought that if she will share about her problems to anyone, that person will either not listen to her, make fun of her or get even more stressed. A year had passed now. And now, both of them were in another class.

Just because of the shortage of that one bench, now also they both were sitting together.

After some months, when they both became parteners for a class project; and started talking and they became friends. Later on... When Months Started Passing, They started to visit each other by going at their houses and now, they were best friends. They started telling their secrets or problems to each other and started ignoring the haters. Everyone was shocked by seeing this. Ishanya helped Shanaya to improve her speaking skills. She helped Shanaya to improve her dressing sense and helped her improve her attitude. Now people did not hate her. They started understanding her. It was all because of Ishanya. Shanaya was very grateful to Ishanya after this.

They were best friends even now. But now, a very strange thing was being seen in their friendship. As usual only, Shanaya used to care a lot about Ishanya but it felt like Ishanya did not even care about her. It felt like Ishanya doesn't want this friendship anymore.

Shanaya just ignored it and felt it's just her misconception. But, is everything a misconception? Ishanya started gossiping about her to her family members and other people. She started ignoring her. She started spreading fake news about her. As if she doesn't even know her. Ofcourse she played a game. She was double faced. Just like other people!

In the same class itself, another girl Emilia took admission in the same school. Ishanya knew Emilia a lot before. (Mentioned in unit 4) As Ishanya and Emilia had studied together in the same school in Karnataka before. After some months, Emilia also became their friend and they all were bestfriends of each other. Shanaya started loving both of them and never complained about Emilia, who was the one who created a wall between their friendship. They had a trio. And Shanaya was very happy about it. But she didn't know that it isn't a trio, It's a betrayal. Suddenly, Shanaya was absent for the next 20 days as her mother passed away because of heart attack. (Mentioned in unit 2). When she came back to school, she saw that Ishanya And Emilia Are now best friends. She hugged them and started crying. But their reaction was like... "Hey! Don't you have manners??"

Shanaya even asked both of them very politely, "What happened?","Why are you behaving like this with me?" "What's wrong? I will help you if you want." But then Ishanya replied, "Shanaya I know you were double faced from the Beginning only. I was just checking you. And now you have proved it right. You are a flipper and you can never be cured. Actually friendship is a beautiful thing which can't be fulfilled by a psycho."

These words hurted her a lot. Although she was emotionally very strong but still couldn't stop herself from crying. She cried for the whole night. And then she suffered with insomnia for weeks. Shanaya was still confused about it. Like... The girls she used to love more than herself, betrayed her. Still Shanaya was thinking that they were just having fun with her because she was very innocent and used to believe that everyone has a good heart. She used to believe that they three are still best friends and they both are just joking or having fun. But Shanaya couldn't realise that the things are not the same now. Shanaya was not a part of Ishanya's and Emilia's priorities but her heart wasn't ready to except it. After some months, Ishanya's birthday came. Shanaya was very excited for her birthday in a week advance only. She wished her with a lot of excitement. She wished her at the first in the Whatsapp group at sharp 00:00 a.m. All the other friends also wished her after seeing Shanaya's message and guess what?? Ishanya thanked each and every one but not Shanaya. She felt so bad after noticing it. And she even messaged her very politely that "You said thank you to everyone but not me!?" Ishanya just saw the message, ignored it, and that's it! She really felt very bad. She cried a lot that day. And that day also, She cried for the whole night and again suffered with insomnia. We can't even imagine that a person's health is becoming worse day by day just because of 2 people! She still thought that Ishanya might be busy and it's not her fault. Months passed! And after some days, Emilia's birthday came. She did the same she did with Ishanya. She got excited, she wished her before everyone else. And guess what!?? Emilia also did the same Ishanya did with Shanaya. Shanaya cried a lot that day. That time also she cried the whole night. Those girls made her cry so much! Even when it wasn't her fault. She still did not realise that both of them are just playing a game with her. She was still not able to recognise their second face. After some days, Shanaya messaged both of them.. But they both started ignoring her. They both started being in their own company and started to make fun of her just like everybody else. Shanaya started realising that they both are just playing a game with her and don't think she is their friend anymore. Shanaya started realising that they both are just double faced and nothing else. As it is said, " 'I love disturbing you' to 'Sorry for disturbing you', Somewhere friendship died" And it was true. From Endless Laughing together to endless crying on one side...

There friendship had really died!

And now,

They were strangers again!

But wait....

What is the story behind it?

Why did Ishanya change immediately?

Was there any particular reason?

Was it all because of Emilia?

Turn the pages!

Read unit-4 and you will come to know about the real one to play the game.

2

Shanaya's Back Story

Shanaya belonged to a middle class family. She had a small family and used to live with her parents and her younger brother. She was considered ugly by the other people as she had a dark complexion, short hair, a short height. She hated herself just because of her looks and because of the financial conditions of her home. She got raised in a poor family and she knew the value of money.

Just because of the situations, she became very mature. Mature than anything else. Her shoes used to be torn and she used to study with second hand books. Because of which, everyone else used to make fun of her. She had never been to a 5-star hotel or restaurant. To visit or to eat something in a restaurant was just like a dream for her. Ofcourse, the financial condition of her family was not good. Because of which she couldn't fulfill her dream. Still she had a lot of interest in studies. It was her dream to provide her parents all the happiness by the money she would earn after growing up. As she used to feel very bad when her parents cried because of the condition of their house. Not even only looks or the financial conditions, But she was stressed by another thing: Her mother's health!

From 6 months, her mother was having some problem in her heart. She sometimes used to get chest pain suddenly and her heartbeat wasn't in control. It was usually high. When they visited the doctor with her mother, the doctor said that they will have to pay him a very huge amount for the surgery of her mother's heart otherwise she can suddenly die anytime. Now, because they couldn't afford the money for her mother's operation, they started to take care of her. Shanaya and her father were very stressed about this but they didn't inform Shanaya's brother about it as he wasn't mature enough. Shanaya had to some of the house hold chores by herself because her mother wasn't well. Because of all these chores, Shanaya couldn't get the time to study or for any other activities. Shanaya was mature enough to understand all this. Ofcourse, The situations made her do so. She was not considered beautiful by people and her uniform also used to be in a very bad condition as it was old and cheap and that's why no one was a friend of hers. She tried very hard making friends but everybody used to ignore her and made fun of her. Many times she tried to commit suicide but failed. Maybe god wanted her to bear all this. She was a kind, friendly and helpful girl. Everybody even in the school used to treat her in a very ill manner as her father was not able to pay the huge amount of fee at once. Her fee used to be pending for months. Because of which her classmates started to make fun of her. And she started cursing herself like.."Why Am I Even Supposed To Live?" She wanted to become a very successful doctor after growing up so that she can do surgeries of the poor people who can't afford much money for the surgeries but everyone used to make fun of her and say "You can't even read properly, How will you become a doctor..?"

Her mother's condition was very critical and now the only thing which could save her was prayers.

This wasn't enough. Just because of the dark complexion of hers, her relatives and even parents used to blame her.

She used to believe that if they will get money, half of their problems will be solved very easily!

3

Ishanya's back story

She belonged to a very high class family. She had a small family and used to live with her parents and her elder brother who was 6 years elder than her. Her father was the manager of a very big company and her mother was a trainer of the biggest gym in the city. She had a lot of arrogance because of all the money they had and ofcourse a lot of fame for the same. She was considered very beautiful by people just because she had long hair, a very good height, long eyelashes, a fair complexion and a clear skin. She used to take care of herself very nicely. She used to workout, used to be hydrated and had a proper routine. She did all of this with her mother who was a trainer in the biggest gym in the city. Whenever she went to a function, event or a party, she used to wear very expensive and beautiful dresses. She was an introvert and didn't like being the centre of attention. She didn't like talking to anyone or participate in a game or activity. She just used to enjoy her own company the most and not anything else. She was very rude to people showing she is beautiful but still she used to remain quiet. She was a very shy girl. She used to be so shy even to ask for help. Everybody in the class used to overcare for her just because she belonged to a high-class family. She didn't use to say it, but she didn't like all that. She hated people, physical touch and getting attention. And that's why whenever someone tried to talk to her, she would just either walk away or talk rudely. Everybody wanted to be friends with her as she was rich and beautiful. But because of her arrogance and interests, she used not to talk to anyone and used to say, "I am alone, but happy." No one knew that deep down she also needs help. She needed love. She was also very depressed inside. She was very tensed because of her dead dog "Brucy" who died 2 years ago. It was the only reason behind her rudeness. As it is said... "Situations change people. Some become rude, some become silent!"

These situations might not really matter that much to us. But they do... To Ishanya.

Let the whole story be known to you:-

Before Brucy died, Ishanya used to be a soft, kind and an immature girl. Every wish of hers used to be fulfilled by her parents as she was the youngest. Brucy was adopted by their family when Ishanya was just 4. She had an elder brother. Her elder brother was 6 years elder than her. As her parents were really busy in their companies and gym, the only one left for her to spend time... Was her brother. Her brother always used to be very busy because of his school projects and homework because of which he could never spend time with his sister. Being the youngest in the family, she really wanted someone to talk to, play with, eat with and have fun with.

From the day she was 4 and got her first pet, she got attached to it. She used to love Brucy more than anything. As Brucy was the only one with whom she used to play with and have a little fun with. After Brucy died, a lot of change was being seen in her behaviour. Her brother started studying abroad after completing the school so he couldn't get a clue of it but her parents also noticed the change. Her parents really wanted to talk to her about it but it wasn't their fault. Whenever they tried to take out time from their busy schedule and tried to talk to her, she used to shout, fight and just run away.

Not just this, a slight change in her appetite was seen too. She started eating less, and she now didn't even talk to her parents.

For Ishanya, money wasn't everything. She believed that money alone cannot buy happiness. Just like how money alone couldn't get her Brucy, all the love Brucy gave her and the memories again turn into alive moments.

4
Let's know about it!

It was just a game played by both of them.

Emilia wasn't the only one to play this game.

Well, Emilia And Ishanya both were interested to play the game and did. They both knew each other a lot before. Their attachment was the loveliest attachment people could see.

Since younger classes only, they were best friends. But in the next class, Ishanya's father had to transferred to Rajasthan and Ishanya had to leave her bestfriend (Emilia) in Karnataka only. They both started being in touch with the help of mobile phones and some small get togethers. When Emilia took admission in the same school in Jaipur, Ishanya didn't inform Shanaya about it. She lied to her. She started paying less attention to her. And the reason for all that happened with Shanaya was nothing but Emilia and her gossips. Ishanya and Emilia, when were talking; Emilia came to know that Ishanaya also secretly hates Shanaya. As Emilia and Ishanya belonged to a very upper-class family, they didn't used to understand the culture of Shanaya's family, Shanaya's Eating habits, her talking habits, even her way of holding a pen. As it was all different from the habits upper class people.

When Ishanya's family got transferred to Jaipur and Ishanya met Shanaya, she suddenly told Emilia that she secretly hates Shabaya. As Ishanya hated Shanaya; she told everything to Emilia. Like... She hates her. It is her helplessness to sit and talk with her. When Ishanya and Shanaya became friends, then some positive image of Shanaya was still there in Ishanya's mind. But, here comes the actual, real.. one to play the game and disturb the whole thing - Emilia.

Let's talk about her now!

She started provoking Ishanya about Shanaya. Like spreading fake news about her or telling Ishanya that Shanaya says bad about you or tells people not to love you. Later, when Emilia took admission in the same school, Shanaya helped her more than anything she could do. As they had a trio.. A fake trio! The trio which Ishanya and Emilia both knew is fake but Shanaya couldn't recognise about it. And when she even got the sign, she ignored it and couldn't recognise why. Shanaya used to help both of them in every way she could. She used to share her stationary with both of them. Emilia told Ishanya that Shanaya is not a good person.

"People like her, who speak politely are usually double-faced." Said Emilia!

At some point, Emilia was also right, but not everybody is same. And Shanaya wasn't one of them.

Now, to convince Ishanya; that she is right and is giving her the best advice; she told her back story.

See everyone is depressed.

Some show it.. Some don't..!

Same was with Emilia. She just didn't show it and had hidden her story but now it was time for her to lessen her

stress and burden. Ofcourse, good days do come!
To know her back story, visit unit-5!

5

Emilia's Back story

Just like Ishanaya and unlike Shanya, She belonged to a high-class family.

She had a joint family and used to live with her parents and grandparents. She was the only child and didn't have any sibling. Because of which she used to feel very alone and had no one to spend her time with.

Before Jaipur, she used to live in Karnataka. Her father also had to transfer because of his business to Jaipur.

Because of which she could get a chance to meet her bestfriend Ishanya. That was when she met Shanaya for the first and Ishanya for the second time after a break. She had curly hair, beautiful eyes, dimples and a good height. Even after being beautiful, she was insecure. She wasn't rude but she wasn't even kind. She was an extrovert and loved parties. She loved making new friends and talking to people. She had a very unique weakness and it was:-

She could not cry easily. And for her parents, whenever she cried, it was shocking. Actually.. It was a sign, that something bad has happened to their daughter. But her parents were not like other parents. Her parents never supported Her. Her parents never used to be by her side.

She used to iron her clothes by herself. And even at times, she had to prepare her lunch box for the school by herself. Her parents were never ready to talk to her and know about her feelings. Her mother was very much into kitty parties because of which her mother was never aware of her child. She was the only child in the family. But still she never wanted to be treated like a princess. Yes but she really liked being the centre of attention.

Her father, who was a business man, could never take out time to spend with his family.

She used to be very sad when her friends told her about how they share each and everything with their parents.

Like Ishanya, even she didn't like to study. She was very good at painting and she wanted to become an artist after growing up. But her parents were always against her choice and her grandparents were busy in their works. Her grandfather loved to worship God and he used to spend most of his time either in the temple or at his friends' place. And her grandmother loved knitting and she used to spend most of her time in knitting socks, caps and sweaters for Emilia. Emilia was grateful for her joint family but a little ungrateful for her parents who never supported her unlike other parents.

She used to believe that a little support from her parents could fix a lot of things and somewhere... She used to believe the right thing.

6
Shanaya's Future

After all this happened, Shanaya started not to talk to anyone or be friends with anyone. She just started focusing on her carrier and stopped talking to people. All the students used to call her "the quiet kid" but she started to ignore all of them and focus on her studies. She started getting top position in every class of hers.

Years passed and passed. All the students were now divided because of their different streams. Shanaya was now divided from the trio too. Shanaya stepped into the PCB stream as she wanted to become a heart-specialist (cardiologist) after growing up. The main reason behind being a cardiologist was her mother. As her mother died because of heart disease just because they couldn't afford that huge amount of money and couldn't manage to get her a surgery. Shanaya wanted to save lives after growing up and wanted to make everybody happy. After being a pass-out from school, she studied in a university in Jaipur only. As her father didn't have much money to send her somewhere else to study. While studying only, she started giving tutions to small children and started collecting money for her studies. Her father also worked day and night just to pay the fee of her education. She was very tensed what if her father's money and hardwork gets wasted?, What if she fails the exam? But she practiced day and night and now, She had passed her exam with a good rank and she is finally a good heart specialist. A cardiologist. Now she is an expert in heart surgeries. She even performs surgeries for free for people who can't afford much money for the surgery. Her dream to provide her father and brother the best life has been finally fulfilled. She takes them to a restaurant by her own money. Her dream finally comes true to have lunch at a restaurant and she is finally living a happy life now.

Shanaya made us realise:-

No matter how bad the situations are. No matter how bad the financial condition is.

No matter how badly you miss your parent, you are still strong and brave enough to fight all that and do something great. You are strong enough to make your loved ones proud and make your loved one's dream come true. See everybody suffers with problems. Everybody misses someone in their life. But it doesn't mean that we will give up. Is giving up this easy? No. Not at all. And we are so lucky to have the opportunity to do something big and make our parents proud. They have been tired of solving theirs as well as our problems. And now it's time for us to solve their problems.

Be Strong!

7

Ishanya's future

Even after all this, there wasn't any change in Ishanya's behaviour or anything else. She was still arrogant and depressed.

As Ishanya didn't have any interest in studies, there wasn't any improvement in her academic skills after growing up. She opted for the Arts stream (Humanities) as she wanted to become a fashion designer after growing up. Her painting teacher really liked her designs and her way of thinking. Her friends and cousins liked her unique carrier choice and always used to appreciate her. Her parents were very happy when they came to know about her hidden talent. They used to appreciate her drawing skills and thinking skills.

And now, it was a great chance for Ishanya:-

One day, there was a competition in Jaipur itself for the whole city. It was not of anything else but fashion designing. Here, Ishanya got the chance to prove herself. She got the chance to show her hidden talent to other people too. Ishanya's school also participated in that competition and so Ishanya did. She was very tensed and excited for the competition. And guess what? Ishanya got the first prize in the fashion designing competition and she was even given the title 'Best Fashion Designer In The City'. She was so happy and their parents conducted a very big party for the same. Now, the only stress left with Ishanya wasn't of anything else but her future. She started worrying if she couldn't become a good fashion designer after growing up. But she worked day and night for the same. And then:-

After growing up, she first completed her studies in abroad and after receiving her degrees from the University, she got into fashion designing. She worked so hard to become a fashion designer. In the starting it was a little difficult for her but later she got good at this. And after becoming successful, there was a change in her behaviour. She finally realised her mistake of being arrogant. She realised how hard it is to earn money and she started to respect people and even the money earned by her parents. She designed her first dresses for her parents who were always by her side. She got so happy and now she is finally a very famous fashion designer.

Ishanya made us realise:-

Yes, Situations Do Change. But sometimes, it's only for our good. If bad time has come, so we will get over it and surely good time will also come. But not without hardwork. The only thing needed if we want good situations is, working hard!

That's what hardwork is!

Not only money can do everything. Hardwork is always needed if we want to achieve something great.

Even if you have all the money, it's not possible to achieve your goal because that's what a goal is all about. People don't see the struggle behind the money or beauty. People just see our success and judge us on the basis of the same.

So, it's better to not blame the situations and do hardwork instead. Because if you've decided, you can achieve it and you will surely do.

Do Hardwork!

8
Emilia's future

After all this, she still had a lot of friends and no Change in her extroverty behaviour. She also opted for the Arts stream (Humanities) as she wanted to become an artist after growing up at any cost. After completing her school, she didn't complete her studies in a university or something because of which there were a lot of fights in her house. Her parents and even she started worrying about her future. But she had trust in herself. She filled a lot of forms for becoming an artist and she got selected in only two of them. When she went to give the competition/exam for the same, she failed both the times. And now, her parents again got the chance to prove her wrong and prove that she can't do anything. But the only thing worked there wasn't anything else but trust. She didn't trust anyone. Well... She trusted herself. She filled more forms and this time not by her parents' money but her own savings. It was really very difficult for her to do so but by having the hope that I can do it, I am trying to do it and one day, for sure I'll finally do it, She won! She won in the battle of life. She won in the competition of her life. After being successful, now she never wishes to gain attention by everybody. Because that's what being mature and improvement is!

And now,

Emilia made us realise:-

Even if everybody is against you, you should... Actually you can never leave your side. You have to trust in yourself because nobody else is going to do it for you. If you start ignoring what people say about you and start to trust, have faith in yourself; you can surely achieve your goal a lot easier. But if you will take care of everybody and everything people have said about you, then the hardest thing to do is nothing but winning. You have to love yourself because love is the fuel of a person and the person who can love you like the best is not anyone other but you... Yourself! The only one to be a part of your priorities should be you, yourself. Other people are too busy to prioritise you so better do it yourself, achieve your goals and live happily!

Trust in yourself!

Author's Experience

If we talk about my experience, it's quite interesting. Not only because it was the first time I wrote a story but also because it was the first time I'm motivating someone. See, whenever I feel low, I don't need anyone to motivate me because the way I motivate myself is better than anyone else doing so. (At least for me it is).

Not only this, but selecting the book covers was interesting as well as confusing. Getting to choose only one cover from all those beautiful covers is quite difficult. I get excited over very small things and this book, it was such a big thing for me. Before even deciding what to write, I got excited about my book. And then.. ideas started to come in my dreams. I think it's the most beautiful experience till now of mine. I personally enjoyed writing this book very much and I hope that you also enjoyed while reading it.

Thank you so much! For reading this book!

Main Message Tried To Convey Through The Book

See, as you read the book, you might feel that it was the fault of the third one. Actually it was. But not everybody is wrong. See, everybody has some plus points and some minus points in their personality. But it doesn't mean that if you notice the minus points first, the person is bad. Everybody in this world is good and everybody understands each other. Everybody suffers with pain and because of pain, there is a change in their behaviour.

Even though it can be difficult, but there are instances when you must separate from someone special in your life just because they have found someone better. And then, you get used to moving on. But some people around you might think that suicide is the option to get out of this pain or suicide will be the best so that they don't have to bear the pain anymore. But it isn't true. Suicide neither solves any problem nor kills your pain. It just kills the happiness of your loved ones and passes your pain to your loved ones. Do you really want to make your loved ones sad? Do you really want to kill their happiness? I'm sure you don't want to.. Hence proved, suicide isn't the option. It's the worst choice anyone could make. If you are really sad or if it's getting too heavy on the heart, just talk to someone. You will feel better. Just be strong because that's what you're. Just do hardwork! Get out of your comfort zone and do as much hardwork as you can. Never lose hope! Because hope isn't something to be loosed. If you really wanna lose something, then lose your pain and burden by trusting in yourself and loving yourself.

And it doesn't mean that you will forget being happy or lose hope. Because that's not what you're. You are a strong person. And you are the best whoever you are. Sadness is just like a small test in life. And learning to handle the sadness and situations with maturity is really hard. But you can surely do it. And you will do it!

Also, if anyone says that you can't do it or you don't have enough guts to do so, prove them wrong. You should have faith in yourself. Even if everybody is against you, you.. Yourself have to be by your side. Because anyone can leave you anytime. Because that's what life is. But it doesn't mean that you will leave yourself too. Don't be left lonely. Love yourself not because you should, just because you deserve it!

Be Strong!
Do Hardwork!
Trust in yourself!

Message From The Key Characters

Shanaya:- Be Strong!

If you're not strong physically, mentally and emotionally; then you can't do or achieve anything. Sorrows are gonna come and go. People are gonna come and go. Money is gonna come and go. But for how long are you gonna regret? Be strong and face your problems. And show life, how brave you are! Be strong! Everything is gonna be alright!

Ishanya:- Do Hardwork!

If you're not getting out of your comfort zone, then also you can't do or achieve anything. Laziness doesn't bring success. You know why? Because life gives the chance to only some people to win. And if laziness could bring success, then everybody would be so much successful. And that's not what success is. Do hardwork while thinking, designing, or doing anything. Do hardwork! Success will come to you on its own!

Emilia:- Trust in yourself!

Trusting yourself is a hundred times better than trusting other people with whom you don't even have some hope about when they can leave you or not. Remember who picked you up when you felt the most down? It was you yourself. Those people who used to say will never leave you, even they did. When you were going through a bad phase. And the only person left with you that time was just you.. yourself!

Trust in yourself! You're surely gonna achieve it!